This Jazz Man

This

KAREN EHRHARDT

Pictures by
R. G. ROTH

Harcourt, Inc.

Orlando   Austin   New York   San Diego   Toronto   London

For my mother,
Dorothy Mae Williams (1928–2003);
my husband, David; and the Revisionaries
—K. E.

For Cassidy and Grace
—R. G. R.

THIS JAZZ MAN RECORDINGS

Library of Congress Cataloging-in-Publication Data
Ehrhardt, Karen.
This jazz man/Karen Ehrhardt;
illustrated by R. G. Roth.
p. cm.
Summary: Presents an introduction to jazz music and nine
well-known jazz musicians, set to the rhythm of the traditional
song, "This Old Man." Includes brief facts about each musician.
[1. Jazz—Fiction. 2. Musicians—Fiction. 3. African Americans—
Fiction. 4. Stories in rhyme.] I. Roth, Robert, 1965- ill. II. Title.
PZ8.3.E297Th 2006
[E]—dc22   2004021094
ISBN-13: 978-0-15-205307-9   ISBN-10: 0-15-205307-7

First edition
H G F E D C B A

Manufactured in China

This BOOK belongs TO

This Jazz Man

Name

_____

Nº 591965   Nº 591965

ADMIT ONE
37

The illustrations in this book were done in mixed media collage
and printmaking on watercolor paper.
The display type was created by R. G. Roth.
The text type was set in NeutraText.
Color separations by Colourscan Co. Pte. Ltd., Singapore
Manufactured by South China Printing Company, Ltd., China
This book was printed on totally chlorine-free Stora Enso Matte paper.
Production supervision by Jane Van Gelder
Designed by Scott Piehl and April Ward

This jazz man, he plays one, **1**

He plays rhythm with his thumb,

With a Snap! Snap! Snazzy-snap!

Give the man a hand,

This jazz man scats with the band.

DOO-AAHAAH!

2

This jazz man, he plays two,

He makes music with his shoes,

With a **Tap-tap! Shuffle-slap!**

Give the man a hand,

This jazz man stomps with the band.

shuffle-step! shim-

This jazz man, he plays three, **3**

He plays congas tween his knees,

With a **Bippity-bop! Poppity-pop!**

Give the man a hand,

This jazz man pounds with the band.

Slap! Pop-pop!

"Now you're Cookin'!"

This jazz man, he plays four,

He conducts 'em through the score,

With a "One, and-a two, and-a—"

Give the man a hand,

This jazz man, he leads the band.

Beeep-bamp-bamp! Bop-bop! Beeee-AAAW

5

This jazz man, he plays five,

He plays bebop, he plays jive,

With a Beedle-di-bop! Bebop!

Give the man a hand,

This jazz man blows with the band.

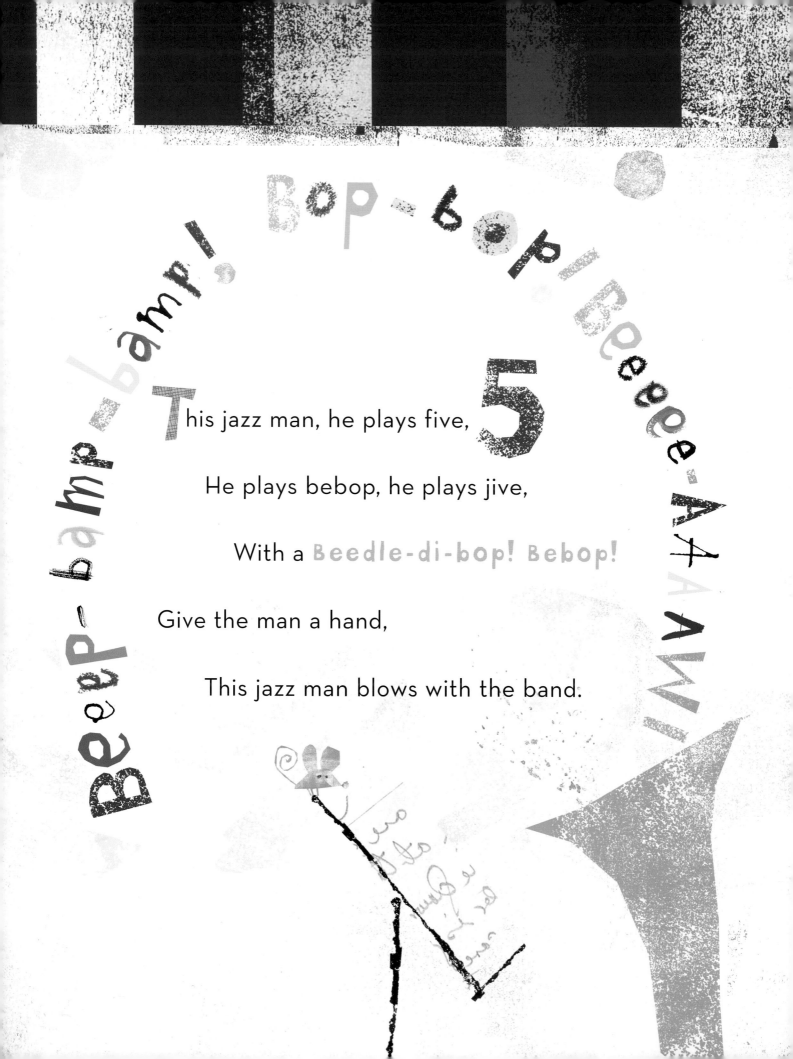

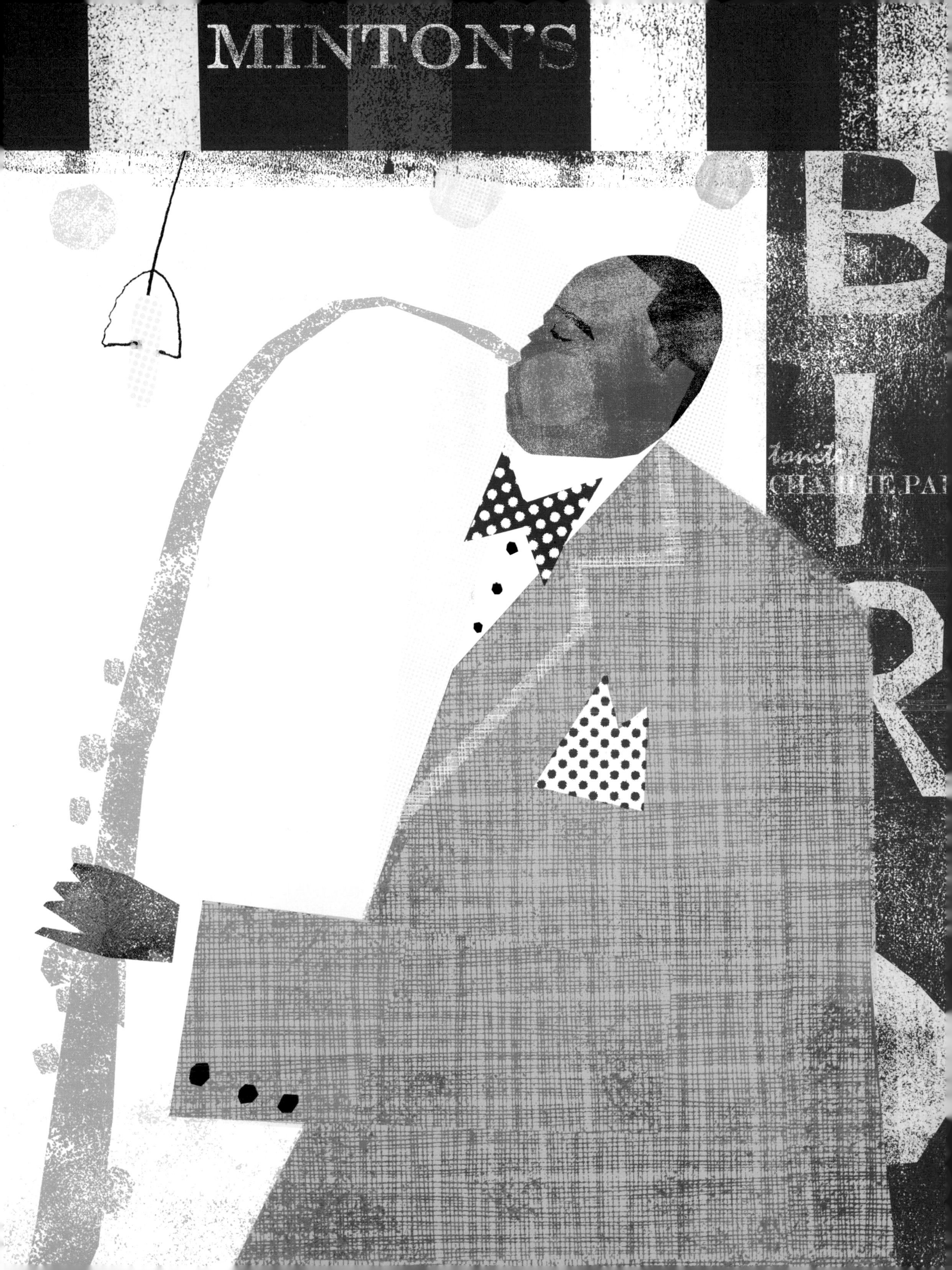
MINTON'S
BIR

This jazz man, he plays six,

He plays solos with his sticks,

With a Bomp-bomp! Bubbuda-bomp!

Give the man a hand,

This jazz man beats with the band.

6

Bubbuda Bubbuda Bubbuda BOmp!

doot-doot! Toot-Toot!

This jazz man, he plays seven, **7**

He plays notes that rise to heaven,

With a Toot-toot! Doodly-doot!

Give the man a hand,

This jazz man wails with the band.

Dink! Dinkle- dink- dink!

This jazz man, he plays eight,

He plays keys—all eighty-eight,

With a Tink-plink! Plinkle-dink!

Give the man a hand,

This jazz man swings with the band.

Thimp dumple thump

This jazz man, he plays nine, **9**

He plucks strings that sound divine,

With a **Thimp-thump! Dumple-thump!**

Give the man a hand,

This jazz man jams with the band.

These jazz men, they play ten,

We beg them to play again,

With an "Encore! We want more!"

Give them all a hand,

These jazz men

1   2   3   4

make one great band!

5   6   7   8   9

Playing **1**, from New Orleans, Louisiana . . .
Louis "Satchmo" Armstrong
(1900–1971)

Easily the most influential musician of the twentieth century, Armstrong revolutionized jazz by *improvising*, or making up tunes as he went along. Not only did he create new melodies through inventive trumpet solos—as in "West End Blues"—he even improvised when singing. This kind of nonsense singing is called scat, and gravel-voiced Armstrong made it popular with his recording of "Heebie Jeebies." The undisputed ambassador of jazz, Satchmo got the whole world swinging!

Playing **2**, from Richmond, Virginia . . .
Bill "Bojangles" Robinson
(1878–1949)

Robinson made music—and history—by tapping his toes with a style and speed never seen before. Some of his signature steps, like the up-and-down-stairs routine, continue to be performed by tap dancers today. A star of the stage and screen, Robinson appeared in movies such as *Stormy Weather* opposite Lena Horne, and *The Little Colonel* with Shirley Temple. Ever light on his feet, Robinson celebrated one birthday by tapping down Broadway sixty-one blocks—one block for each year!—and into the theater where he was appearing that night.

Playing **3**, from Havana, Cuba . . .
Luciano "Chano" Pozo y González
(1915–1948)

Pozo was a celebrated *conguero*, or conga player, and composer of carnival songs in Cuba when he moved to New York City in 1946 and began playing with jazz giant Dizzy Gillespie. Pozo's sizzling beats transformed Gillespie's bebop into Cubop, a blend of Afro-Cuban rhythms and jazz. Marveling at Pozo's ability to dance, sing, and play simultaneously in different rhythms, Gillespie said, "I never knew how he could do that." Hear some of Pozo's fiery drumming on "Manteca" and "Tin Tin Deo.".

Slap!

Pop-pop!

Bop~bop!Beeee!

Playing **4**, from Washington, D.C. . . .
Edward Kennedy "Duke" Ellington
(1899–1974)

Ellington was a gifted pianist, yet it was together with his orchestra that he was most dazzling. A preeminent composer and conductor, Ellington tailored his sophisticated musical pieces to each of his dozen or so musicians, while also anticipating how all of the instruments would sound in unison. Ellington wrote nearly two thousand compositions and in 1969 was awarded the highest civilian honor, the Presidential Medal of Freedom. Listen to Ellington's big band in full swing on songs like "It Don't Mean a Thing" and "Take the 'A' Train."

Playing **5**, from Kansas City, Kansas . . .
Charlie "Bird" Parker
(1920–1955)

A legendary jazz soloist, Parker played the saxophone with an unmatched blend of eloquence, subtlety, and exhilarating speed. He would alter the accents and phrasing of a well-known song so completely that it was no longer recognizable. Together with Dizzy Gillespie, Parker created the complex melodies and unpredictable harmonies called bebop. Known for practicing a tune in several keys to learn it inside and out, Parker once said, "Master your instrument, master the music, and then forget all that —— and just play." On songs like "Ko Ko" and "Scrapple from the Apple," he makes it sound so easy.

Playing **6**, from Pittsburgh, Pennsylvania . . .
Art "Bu" Blakey
(1919–1990)

Blakey was an innovative drummer whose *press rolls* (leaning an elbow on the drum's surface to change the intonation) were imitated by many. Blakey's explosive style was the backbone of hard bop jazz classics like "Moanin'" and "Drum Thunder." Combining bebop improvisation with a driving blues backbeat, hard bop featured lengthy solos played by various musicians. When the soloists ran out of ideas, Blakey would play new rhythms to inspire them. Over a span of almost forty years, dozens of young musicians *earned their chops*, or learned their craft, as members of Blakey's band, the Jazz Messengers.

Playing **7**, from Cheraw, South Carolina . . .
John Birks "Dizzy" Gillespie
(1917–1993)

Gillespie was a trumpet player without equal. Finding swing music too predictable, he and his comrade Charlie Parker started a jazz uprising with bebop. Fast and furious, bebop challenged listeners with complex rhythms and wild improvisation, giving Gillespie a showcase for his spectacular skill. "Salt Peanuts" and "A Night in Tunisia" are two of his quintessential tunes. Not only did Gillespie have a trademark look—goatee, glasses, beret, and ballooning cheeks—his horn was also a one-of-a-kind. Someone accidentally bent the bell (the flared end) of his trumpet, and Gillespie liked the trumpet's new sound so much, he played it—and ones like it—for the next thirty years.

Playing **8**, from Harlem, in New York City...
Thomas Wright "Fats" Waller
(1904–1943)

Waller was a master of *stride piano*, which involves the left hand keeping a constant, rumbling beat and the right playing light, bouncy melodies. Equally talented at composing, he wrote and recorded hundreds of songs. Waller was also a popular entertainer, performing in nightclubs, theater productions, and films including *Stormy Weather* with Bill "Bojangles" Robinson. Setting his bowler hat at a jaunty angle, he'd roll his eyes and make faces while singing and *tickling the ivories*. Waller's rambunctious wisecracks during live broadcasts of songs like "Your Feet's Too Big" won him millions of fans and colorful nicknames such as "Radio's Harmful Little Armful."

Playing **9**, from Watts, in Los Angeles ...
Charles "Baron" Mingus
(1922–1979)

Mingus was a phenomenal bassist—one of the few to reach the ranks of bandleader. Raised on gospel music and classically trained, Mingus learned about jazz firsthand from Armstrong, Parker, and Ellington. Working with these master musicians, together with his love of blues and Latin music, inspired Mingus to create a unique sound rich with emotion and personal meaning. Later he founded the Jazz Workshop, a group that promoted young composers, and started his own company to publish and protect his original pieces. Whether honoring his mentor, saxophonist Lester Young, with songs including "Goodbye Pork Pie Hat," celebrating his faith in "Wednesday Night Prayer Meeting," or protesting inequality with "Fables of Faubus," Mingus always had a story to tell.

The End

Hope you enjoyed the SHOW.